the lonely pine

Published in 2011 by Creative Editions   P.O. Box 227, Mankato, MN 56002 USA

Creative Editions is an imprint of The Creative Company.

Designed by Rita Marshall

Printed in Italy

Library of Congress Cataloging-in-Publication Data

Frisch, Aaron. The lonely pine / by Aaron Frisch; illustrated by Etienne Delessert.

Summary: A small pine that is Earth's northernmost tree experiences a year's worth of Arctic

sights, changes, and hardships, including the aurora borealis, vast animal migrations, and brutal cold.

ISBN 978-1-56846-214-1

[1. Pine—Fiction. 2. Trees—Fiction. 3. Animals—Arctic regions—Fiction. 4. Nature—Fiction.

5. Tundras—Fiction. 6. Arctic regions—Fiction.] I. Delessert, Etienne, ill. II. Title.

PZ7.F9169Lo 2011   [E]—dc22   2010028643   CPSIA: 120110PO11407

First edition

9 8 7 6 5 4 3 2 1

Aaron Frisch & Etienne Delessert

the lonely pine

Creative Editions

The pine stood alone.

It had grown where it should not.

The air was too bitter.

The ground too solid. Earth's crown too close.

And yet, there it stood.

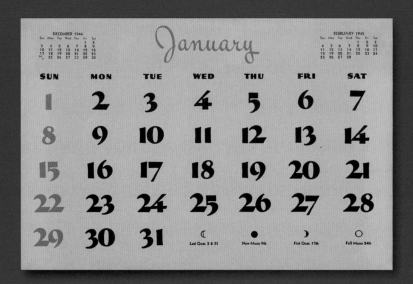

The pine was small.
High as an ox beard, never to be taller.
The wind threw daggers of ice that had shorn the tree ragged.
But the pine knew nothing of other trees.

JANUARY 1945
Sun Mon Tue Wed Thu Fri Sa
1 2 3 4 5 6
7 8 9 10 11 12 13
14 15 16 17 18 19 20
21 22 23 24 25 26 27
28 29 30 31

February

MARCH 1945
Sun Mon Tue Wed Thu Fri Sa
1 2 3
4 5 6 7 8 9 10
11 12 13 14 15 16 17
18 19 20 21 22 23 24
25 26 27 28 29 30 31

SUN	MON	TUE	WED	THU	FRI	SAT
☾ Last Quar. 5th	● New Moon 12th	☽ First Quar. 19th	○ Full Moon 26th	1	2 GROUND HOG DAY	3
4	5	6	7	8	9	10
11 EDISON'S BIRTHDAY	12 LINCOLN'S BIRTHDAY	13	14 ASH WEDNESDAY ST. VALENTINE'S DAY	15 SUSAN B. ANTHONY'S BIRTHDAY	16	17
18	19	20	21	22 WASHINGTON'S BIRTHDAY	23	24
25	26	27 LONGFELLOW'S BIRTHDAY	28			

Roots held the tree fast.

Nature allowed it no language.

The lichens and lemmings offered it no fellowship.

The pine could only live.

Live and watch and listen and feel.

And this it did.

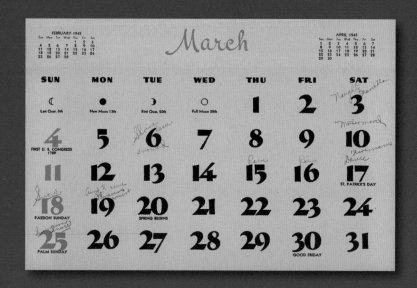

Cold gripped the pine.
Cold that made its limbs creak and needles jangle.
Cold that banished clouds and robbed the land of light.
But the pine endured.

A fox came.
Black eyes and nose on a dim white canvas.
The fox curled beneath the pine's boughs.
For two days, the wind wailed. When it ceased, the fox unfurled.
It disappeared back into white.

The sky burst with trumpeting.

Bright beaks by the thousands rode in on the growing sunshine.
A parade of feathers put the pine in shadow.
Some of the parade landed.
Some of the shadow sailed north.

The earth trembled.
Hot breaths steamed skyward.
A forest of fur encircled the pine,
its branches of horn swirling the steam.
Noses tested needles and moved on.

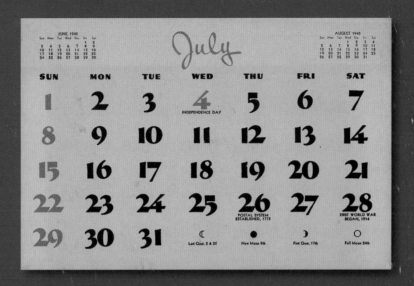

The sun finally showed its full face.
Green returned. Glorious green.
With red and yellow splashed here, blue painted there.
The sun stayed and loomed low, as if to admire.

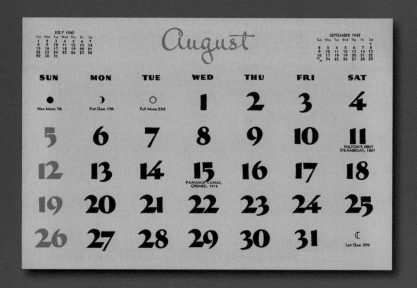

The air buzzed.

Winged bugs and tiny biting things hurried to live.
Moths fluttered against the pine like the ghosts of snowflakes.
Night fell hard.
The buzz hushed.

AUGUST 1945
Sun Mon Tue Wed Thu Fri Sat
            1   2   3   4
5   6   7   8   9   10 11
12 13 14 15 16 17 18
19 20 21 22 23 24 25
26 27 28 29 30 31

September

OCTOBER 1945
Sun Mon Tue Wed Thu Fri Sat
    1   2   3   4   5   6
7   8   9   10 11 12 13
14 15 16 17 18 19 20
21 22 23 24 25 26 27
28 29 30 31

SUN	MON	TUE	WED	THU	FRI	SAT
		● New Moon 6th	☽ First Quar. 14th	○ Full Moon 21st	☾ Last Quar. 28th	1
2	3 LABOR DAY	4	5	6	7	8 JEWISH NEW YEAR
9	10	11	12	13	14	15
16	17 CONSTITUTION DAY YOM KIPPUR	18	19	20	21	22
23 30 FALL BEGINS	24	25	26	27	28	29

The sun retreated.
The colors followed, hunted by the cold.
The world turned silver under black.
Bright stars freckled the sky.
The moon reclaimed its throne.

A weary owl burdened the pine.

The pine wobbled but held.

Bird and tree studied the dark emptiness together.

Somewhere something squeaked.

The owl in silence departed.

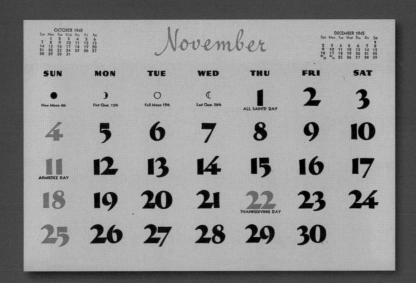

The heavens igníted.
Green fluttered and orange flamed, like memories of warmth long gone.
Purple curtains waved.
The show illuminated unending nights.

Barking dogs came in rows.
A man draped rope on the tree. He set a glove on its peak.
The man leaned on an ax and considered the pine.
Then he took up his things.
The barking slid south.

And so it went for the pine.

No eyes noted if it changed with the seasons.
If it leaned this way or that. If needles were added or lost.

The pine was lonely. But it did not know it.

January

February

March

April

May

June

July

August

September

October

November

December